Table of Contents

Dedication

"Stage Fright"

In dedication to Tony Green for editing on the completion of the piece.

Humility

Hey Humility, you embody my failures while pressing my mental for success.
We've been friends before,
How are you doing?
Your sarcastic remarks hurt the most, this is why we go our separate ways,
You cursed me with a laugh after greeting me with an apology letter of shame.
No, no one ever hears me or bothers to think maybe he tried,
Maybe he gave it all he couldbut, in the moment he was already defeated at the doorstep.
A warrior never stays on his knee's, there are multiple ways to win how will you choose to play.
Scars mean you survived,
Walkin' on a limp toe battlin' self doubt but yet, you are still destined to touch the sky.
Use every lesson as a stepping stone, every win, every loss.
Sit quietly, play dummy if you must but, never give up and if you find yourself

doubting again you are not worthy of that pen you call a sword, triumphant!
Stand up! What are you doing on that ground.
I am disappointed in you.
You admire being pushed to the next level but that last challenge offered no trials,
We won't vent breath, I see you gripping your weapon the wind blowing, giving those lungs baby breaths to breath.
Will you stand up, hmmm?
Speaking from those tongues that laughed at you,
 that pointed fingers,
I am Humility.

Inspired

Words cut from the tongue,
You said you had to go, when I wasn't ready for you to leave,
Had lines of grief over a blank face,
Does having your heart broken mean you age faster,
The tears ran from his lips but not his eyes,
When the words didn't come out,
He didn't speak because, he knew the situation,
An angel had to fly when she got the taste of freedom,
You was the good trapped in a box of bad,
Was this home?
He found serenity in hell, when you smiled time slowed, your presence was tranquil.
I guess, temptation isn't always bad,
It makes me wanna rip my heart from my chest to show you and say this is your piece,
I wouldn't hold you,
You deserve to fly,
So stretch them wings that's been aching to spread across the sky,
You beautiful,
62 years young you been dying for a change who am I to express myself and tell you you shouldn't go,
Only for selfish gain,
You were my peace,

Grandmamma.

Charismatic
I appreciate
Your work
as an
Artist
keep
striving!
!!

Grandmamma

Inspired by the deceased,
The memories brought loneliness as we
celebrated with the food you'd probably make,
Made for us on Easter Sunday or,
Even Saturday noon play warmth on a child's
heart as you watched us go astray,
The suns rays came in to wash our sins away.
A hug as soft as the cotton we got our backs
whipped for, those same whippings from you
taught us we knew better,
Taught the little flower girls that someday they'll
bloom into sophisticated women who would be
the structure of a household while,
The young boys were taught to build the
foundation, to hold up the floor plan.
Grandmamma ,
You was the reason I could have this momma,
That knew me better like the broken jigsaws to a
jokers face,
Momma is the only woman who can ground me,
Who's roots are deep with trained experience.
Her smiles were the beauty to the equivalent of
waterfalls in tropics with doves flying,
She walked across my room in that white gown
just as you did,
I remember fallin', broken bones scabs and all
across the concrete.

You came to my aid sayin' "boy clean yo face, you alive right...?
Dust yourself off and try again," in the words of Aliyah.
If I never bared witness to towers fallin' from the interstate then, I seen lightning striking birthing a blaze to the world when I seen you take your final lay.
I DIDN'T HAVE FLOWERS OR WHTE ROSES THAT DAY!
I did have a Batman action figure
As your body in a casket only made me question why weren't you blinking,
Grandmamma,
I place that action figure in your resting hands,
Just to go looking for it some years later again.

Babygirl In Stilettos

We gon' pay for your body with a conversation,
Baby...
How often has a man called you that and didn't
mean it?
Did you choose this profession or was it forced
under circumstances,
We got a moment for now living by the word like
graffiti to a street,
As if I don't got a home to get to,
As if you don't got customers to please,
What's your background story,
Body as gold as a calf the men selling their souls
for just to pay you,
I'm not judging the fact that you paying debt off
by exposing yourself,
But you are only truly naked when your soul is
revealed,
How many people has seen you skin bare with
clothes on?
I'm lookin pass the Stiletto's and Jimmy Choo's,
If you were Victoria's Secret you'd be the best one
kept,
wrapped in lace every mans fantasy,
Give me a moment,
The reason I ain't answering the phone when it
rings,
The reason you ain't giving it up to nobody,
I heard there was a message in a woman's curves,

Let your womb be the gift,
As you undress slow,
The surprise kept secret from an excited boy on his birthday,
Mouth watering,
Worshiping the sight from a distance but looks ain't everything,
The clock is almost out with the music playing in the background,
The strobes reflecting off your heart like my finger touched the image water rippled,
Intimately from a physical standpoint,
Your mental was inspired,
By a guy who paid you for conversation,
Hat forward, shirt buttoned, pants barely sagging,
But this was your show,
And you fulfilled the case,
Babygirl In Stilettos,
You wanna be there for me to fall back on, when the weight is heavy?
It always feels better when someone understands,

Life Is a Gamble

Life moves at an interesting pace,
Slowly learned to let my mistakes guide me to better waves,
Like that boy on the concrete in a tux with flowers skating to a date on Sunday,
All he had was a Monday's worth of allowance,
He was on his way,
He wanted her to feel special like steak and eggs,
I wanna savor the taste,
For another day to go back too in the archives of my memories when our times pass,
Because, We're young and nothin last forever,
Another lesson life read me after falling to lust,
While attachment watched knowing I'd be back in that same square again, because love is complicated,
We just gon' slow it down here for the moment,

I'm not ready to pass go let me get another chance at the merry go,
As the rounds emptied,
I kinda wish the Ferris was forever empty
So I could put my quarters in and go again,
This is a long road do you wanna show it to me Ms. Oracle
I rolled these dice this time I was looking in some snake eyes,
As the car pulled up slow gotta play the hand that's dealt,
We grabbed the mask every young black male,
Should never feel,
My boys cocked the guns with the silver sun turning the shine over to the golden moon,
This what we do,
We ran to the clerk,
He locked the store doors
My boy said, "freeze you move I'll blow the sneeze off your face,"
We moved quick unlocked the bronze hinges into the cash register we went,
Only a good g 4 of us that's about 250 each
But, its what you spend it on,

Tasteful or wasteful,
Lets roll again,
This time I'm lookin at a seven,

Women Wants Pt. 1

Stop,
Legs wide open,
Fiendin' for more,
Penetration,
Take this slow,
You might get took for granted,
Tongue so smooth you Felt the serpent,
He talked you off you pants and panties,
Had you fascinated with the fornication he
filled your mind with,
Eyes rollin' back,
You see a bigger picture,
He twirled your twine,
You got lost in the mix,
This just might be it,
See, you never listen
You felt what your eyes saw so your guard
was down,
Not paying attention you just wanted love,
In the chase for it you lost yourself,
Tears for recognition,
You better than this,
At least that's what you thought,
The devil takes shapes amongst the crowd,

You got options so you pick slow,
Oops, hand in the pot another bad apple,
Nobody to patch the scars,
And, you can't fix this with used bandages,
So you went searching again,
As if last nights advice meant nothin'
You said, "your focus was on you because,
there is no "I" in team,"
So, your company is found in ingenuine
arms,
You want something real but, don't know
what real is,
When your worth is missing

Orange Autumn Breeze

Blowing from the autumn tree,
Orange Autumn Breeze,
Bristling knocking down the leaves,
The wind grabs its partner in nature,
She runs they run together,
In a hands held,
From the fire of men burning of black soul
no love for nature,
These physical demons laugh at pain
despair is accompanied,
Though the sun still shines a smile on the
city,
It's beautiful,
That love,
Orange Autumn Breeze,
Blowing from the autumn tree,
Autumn leaves birthing a snow the soot
from the smoke freezes over,
There is a wink of hope,
Warm dancing in the art of compassion,
Two in many one in all,
That dove drops a feather fall signified the
weather,
Orange Autumn Breeze,

Blowing from the Autumn Tree,
There is no love to hold of the one with the
lust for nature in his eyes and everything
natural,
Once again there our tree stands,
Hand and hand with wind,
I am the summer of after life reborn,
Orange Autumn Breeze,
Blowing from the Autumn Tree,

Stage fright

Yea, you got talent,
But, what you gone do with that,
Sweat from the palms an opportunist plays
on prey In these moments,
Make music you a trap nigga,
If you can rhythmize words over stolen
instrumentals
Where is the creativity,
Oh she left about a year ago when they let
the double xls tell them what dope is,
Well I'm dope nigga,
So line em up tell them boys I'm waiting for
a good fade hope the bars is lined up,
I can't level up smoking weed,
Why would I tarnish my mental saying I
think I believe I need,
Let me tell you What I think I believe I need,
I need this thing called stage fright to leave
as eyes bury deep over the words I was
trying,
Maybe they didn't rhyme right when I said
it then it was all twisted up,
Kinda like talkin to that first crush in high
school,

I seen her in the hall before I got on the bus,
I knew she got on the bus because I would exit at the back of the school to walk home to avoid them foos with rags out they pocket,
No, not being judgmental just that there is always a better path so I chose to walk alone knowing that I wasn't alone,
A train track can switch lanes any day so I stuck to my roots going wherever passion took me,
Leading with wonder,
As I got home I noticed the bus on the left side of the street,
There she bee's just what I need like a Lilly, this philly, or daisy maybe got me,
Turning down my hat and wondering if she noticed me as I unpacked my Vegas strap back with 7s on it,
A soft knock on the door took me from my dreams,
There she was before me this black beautiful queen,
But, opportunity brings pressure to sweaty palms

My mind danced as syllables raced from my head to my lips,
I heard me say excuse me and saw myself slam the door,
You make me nervous but it's worth it.
 The mic. Dropped.

Chicago

Chi-ca-go's
I see it comin, I see it comin,
They don' popped something,
Them boys comin'
You
Better
Run
Where death is a signature note for a
person with money, cars and clothes,
You shot fam so I gotta retaliate,
I'ma scholar but the streets that hold me
close is somewhere left in the ghetto's,
Karma blends as my soul flows free
something is calling me,
Wrong place, wrong time, right,
I caught a stray,
Eyes roll back as my life fades,
Car pulls of as the wheel sways,
I woke up in white,
Standing in a room talkin to myself,
While looking down dirty in the mud of
misplaced words and actions that disgrace
my name,
Then I say boy, elevate!

See the murda caused by puppet strings,
A voice is a muh-fucka,
We just wanted to be free,
I woke up feelin' a pain in my forehead,
Blood dripping from my nose,
All the sickness gone,
With dreams,
The conversation unfolds lookin in a mirror
you was on stage,
When we come together we bond strong
they fear us,
Chicago, Chicago!! Chicago!!
It just had to be me,
Never imagined being the boy on stage,
Holdin a mic. Talkin while the people say my
name,
I was just here like yesterday cornflakes in a
bowl where I ate,
Saturday's sense pops left never been the
same,
Cartoons have changed and I cannot get
affection unless my heart is broken,
Along with loneliness when I wear pain on
my sleeve,

They say I am the   piece to keep them together,
Peace...
Drowning in emotion,
This is where in my heart my thoughts are slain,
Why do you burden me,
My heart doesn't answer as I take it and throw it in my chest,
Just to cast it in the Atlantic Sea,
The pain from a ghost behind eye's,
That watch his people slave,
Chicago! Chicago!!
Somewhere walking on sand beaches is where my soul stayed,
Popping fireworks for every name on a rest and peace shirt,
Trapped in a piction of deep regrets of what I coulda did,
Instead I left love where my heart slept,
Why,
Would you wanna murder me,
Staring in the eyes of an assassin,
Told many stories of heartless kills for a dollar,

Sugar is more addictive than crack,
Sweet scents raises desires,
Drugs takes you to the edge of the earth,
Will you take the plunge,
Why do we live this way,

More Worried

More worried bout the police these days,
More worried about my brutha of the same
skin tone aiming at me these days,
 More worried,
That the youth might not see better role
models,
Taking a tole when we escape,
To the cannabis clouds to get our mind off
it,
They say as a black man we endangered,
Like a higher species birthed us to put us
through hell,
Weeding the weak from strong,
Are you the goof in the mirror posing for
the gram or,
You the real deal, like these real niggas they
rap about.
Poet Spit, from the dopest ocean flow from
the crevices of water erupting a volcano
through her legs,
I'm more worried about the police these
days,
Hope these words I pour from my lip,

Would inspire you to be aware of the things we doin,
Along with the influences we cause, blinded by the camouflaged eyes the coated lotus unleashed upon us,
The other day my lil nephew took a shot following the leader,
He said, I wanna be just like you,
Funny how our influences could make us wanna change our life path and watch the words we display on the hardrives of our tongues inflamed,
More worried that you won't get to see,
How great things became,
Because, I out grew you,
Never wanting to be stuck in the mud,
Then, I know my purpose would be slipping,
As self fulfillment slipping down the drain,
Guess I was too worried,

How we got lost in the forest

We can tell stories about how we got lost in the forest,
You took my hand in the dark babygirl,
I didn't see a sight til the lights was off pay attention,
I lost the smooth touch of reality rubbing against you,
It came as mature as nature feels,
She sparked a shine in the dark that blinds me,
The influence I need to push harder,
It's too tough out here to handle alone,
The path is best walked singled out,
Studying myself and my lows like an open book,
Who will I bee,
Embrace thee,
As you slip away, into the night that hugged your dreams dearly,
Where did we go,
Pulling from string and box snap, you're gone,
As the forest grasps us we let go of what we was,

Wrapped up in what we'll be,
We become
As I embrace her naked and bare,
She clinched me,
As the strokes ran from the sands of time
we became each other,
How we got lost in the forest,
She told me don't leave the night held us
stitched together
In the moonlight,
Dance with me, I remember you,
Like you remember me, this vibe is carried
over I'm talkin past life,
You have something to teach me so let the
lessons began,
How we got lost in the forest,
Keep up the forest Is deep,
The only way out is at the end,
You lose your mind and become free,
She lets herself go exploding to me,
How deep is this bond,
I don't think you know,
Let the guitar strings sing the moon called
peace to the sun as the pyramids came,
She showed me,

How we got lost in the forest,

S.A.L.L.Y

Sally,
So along Lyla and Lilly yelled
Comin In from the back side, the dark side
jamming, while the white steady yappin,
Smoky black cars rolling,
They seen it comin,
Lyla dreamed of drive-bys never knew,
Cheeks barely mature eyes of an angel,
Stuck in hell manipulative lands,
Even she can see with her eyes closed she
wanted to help the world,
Growing fifteen Lilly came,
She was sudden like a battle to death,
She ain't trust nothin,
She ran with them boys who played with
toys,
Into trouble she got out of because,
Her looks was innocent to the untrained
vision sally,
So along Lyla and Lilly yelled,
Her boys got caught up everybody lost,
Them niggas from 80 block set them up,
She wanted retaliation, that's how Lilly felt,
Nobody to control the streets Lyla walked,

She called me because she ain't wanna take the trip alone her little brutha needed milk,
So I came only to see Lyla knocked unconscious on the street,
Pants on the side of her shirt ripped off lip busted,
Home is something to be trusted,
We livin weary,
Sally,
So along Lyla and Lilly yelled,
So one day this night after I seen this horrifying thing,
Lilly was coming out of the house on her way to school,
I was fetching the mail
As the car creeped slow,
Aimed the guns, the silence of the morning settled In on the dew, tattooed in blood on the sidewalk,
Guess they was waiting all night to get this one,
But this one had me stuck,
The guns went off,
Doom. DOOM .DOOOMM...
Everything slowed as the guns went,

Her body fell lifeless,
As the light drained from her eyes that weighed hopes of the future,
Sally
So along Lyla and Lilly yelled,
There she layed in the hospital spread,
All I remember is hearing the beeping in dreams,
Which aloud me to travel,
The doctor said, she suffered internal bleeding,
Some how the man who raped her ruptured her spleen,
I can hear her mother screaming not my baby,
Not mine,
I sat back twice two falling victims of the streets two falling victims of the struggle,
Sally,
So along Lyla and Lilly yelled,

Self Conscience

I,

Held up the letter I like his worth was invested in questioning,

I got me when them white guys flipped on the pilgrims we,

Celebrate death like genocide was an investment,

I,

Put my two cents in like this information gon' win me a present,

Present,

As I lace my shoe trynna present myself to a weapon,

Weapon as chemical struck to Flouride makin' mine desensitized,

Bullets in a lab testament,

We, wasn't wearing lab coats our faces was covered,

Black with beanies over it,

Did we really need the rag over the gun like we wasn't already pinned with aggression,

I,

Wasn't there when it happen I was a witness by-standing the conditions

I,
Seen the videos on the news reporter telling us he related to our pigments,
I,
Reminded me to laugh and grip hope to these decisions,
What path is this,
I stood in that room when that dude across the counter screamed don't shoot as my phone rang momma musta been Jesus callin' sayin' come home you got a plate of food if only she knew,
I,
Told me to lower the weapon when time froze usually there is a devil to the left begging as the angel beckoned back in argument,
But, they didn't show,
I,
Seen the whole thing came rushing in as held my brutha back from misdirection,

My Spirit, Her

I had a conversation with me the other day, I said, "I could write a storm and tell the people folktales of old myths they call fibs but what's real ain't. So we heard lies, we will rise within the stone tomb.

Body crafted to fit I lay, until opening my eye and the water came.
The water said, "I seen you the other day setting fires to the gardens you fire starter."
I looked at her and said, "whats a garden of fake roses bloomed than a garden of real pedals in beds which used to be flowers?"

I lie to protect you, the very tomb of a woman's womb us as men we need you. The water cried it started raining she hugged me saying, "I love you." So I left her emotion with no expression. Her waters moved at her exit. I looked to the suns crests peaking over the water I watched awaiting I would never see her again.

Speaking deeply in imaginative thought. I'm thinkin' would I ever so walk alone. Playing with fire you burn unmeaningful without fault I wanted to jump into the drought from this painful sought. Thoughts not suicide I ran the sands of her beaches then, the sun spirit came her rays calmed my eyes in soft chimes her voice went "Oh Pharaoh," she proclaimed seductively. "Why do you ever so dine alone." I watched her craft as day past she laughed, "you're troubled." Her flames flickered and cracked as the air blew calm I ask, "Why do you ray down from the sky's; melting the ground as if the sand couldn't stand your feat? The light you bring to me is beautiful." She said, " would you ever so hold my endless flame so carefully." She gazed into my soul diving into my spirit bonding with my being, "become one with me," she said. "Don't ever let this endless thing go," exclaiming. I looked to the flowers they cried, they witnessed the bond pass materialism she was relentless. She shined bright I couldn't deny looking into her eyes I looked to the ocean waves. "I cannot leave the crest of the heart I left. For, I lied to protect her. For you the truth is I cannot be with you forced to be alone till truly inlove I am because, that love I don't see in you. Justice is not taking advantage of you." I looked to her, "it should satisfy you that I respect you." She looked up a lava formed at the tip of her eye running to her lash remembering our last encounter. She kissed me then whisked away. I cried some other days her flame the flame that burned so effortlessly, cracking against the wind dancing With fine water running a sound formed. I watched the flame flicker day by day I felt their pain.

I took deep breaths feelings my lungs expand the wind came. "Are you here to persuade, I cannot do this anymore." I looked at her knowing I could not escape the sun nor the rain when the wind came. She said, "you're in pain; why do you walk this plain in burden?" I said, "because the burden reminds me of who I am." She said, "why do you hold their spirits close when you can have anything?" I looked at her and said," anything is nothin to me it's not the things she does or the things I seen within this love thing you are all over me. I fall as if my heart has been ripped out of my chest! Wind, you are the air us men need for nutrients of the lungs we need to breath remembering the waters tears, the sunshine's lava. The wind came to me she rose me up staring deeply the infatuation was siting in the moment watching she whispered, "I want you like I want marriage, I want you

like I desire happiness, I want you like I'm committed to you craving you, fiendishly!

I looked in space seeing visions of our happiness swift she is. I said, "I lie, I lie, I cannot share these... (pausing)

she left that's the last of her spirit I saw again.

I returned to my tomb and retain my regret.

I lie, I lie,

My Spirit, Hers

The Boy Who Ran

He looked for love inside a box that he
studied over too many times knowing,
That, these cracks could be fixed if he
wanted to die a little more,
He wouldn't know how long it would take
for him to be reborn
Livin' lygend,
He,
The boy who ran,
When he couldn't stand his tormented
shadow changing faces evil laughs wall
indents the paragraph...
Sentence running on and on,
Sadly this is what happens when the
batteries low on a 2000 model Sedan with
the mileage high,
He couldn't escape the amusement of the
matrix,
So he plugged back in,
Gimme that juice of all the nonsense,
He not talkin robots,
He,
A fallen victim of a computer chipped in his
brain if it ever decays,

His memory could be displayed on a slide show,
After seeing his father beat his mother,
Slow it down now,
Letting go is a process,
Freedom from traumatical instances,
Intensely met,
He looked for love inside a box that he studied over,
That these cracks could be fixed if he wanted to die,
He turned a liquor rage on him,
Is this the same person I dearly love the confusion burning his eyes with tearing, screams down his cheeks,
Questioning,
Showing his true self In the dark,
The door closes,
How could this be?
So he ran,
As the rain came down on the boy who ran,
He came to a restaurant his grandma took him before he was twelve he was six,

Until that man exposed the hate for good In his eyes selfishly taking a kindred spirit from a much needed world,
Dreaming she sends premonitions in his sleep Ms. Oracle speaks to him, No, silence his eyes get wide,
These rainy days never stopped coming,
She loved him with the time spent
He was at the vending machine asking God for another go of it,
Quarters in hand,
He didn't reply,
Crying on the bench Outside the boy sat,
In a muscle shirt and sweats all wet,
The boy who ran,
It only took him a millisecond within the one he caught his breath thinking to himself,
He cried more on the run to a far off bridge,
A far, far place,
Where everybody could see him but nobody watched,
The rain raged the waves swayed,
Along the cheeks of his face,
Water fell into that sea,

He took one last look at the city,
Then asked, "why I can't just be free no more running,"
He stepped further to the edge,
To see his future flashing in-front of him,
He plunged,
Falling, boy who ran,
His body picked up speed,
The air breezed down his face,
More peaceful than anything he felt before,
He hit the water,
God!
He woke up,
In a light shed white room with something that looked like it had wings,
But he couldn't see,
It said, "rest easy,"
The voice sounded familiar,
Angel come to me angel don't run from me,
Young man!
Angel!
Grandmama,
He was 12 then,he's 20 now,
In his head he's still the boy who ran,

Made in the USA
Columbia, SC
16 March 2019